FORTUNE IN MEN'S EYES

AN AMERICAN FAMILY™ BOOK FIVE: 1853

Fortune in Men's Eyes

S. D. JONES

FEARON EDUCATION
a division of
David S. Lake Publishers
Belmont, California

Cover illustrator: Nanette Biers

ISBN 0-8224-4755-X
Library of Congress Catalog Card Number: 88-81524
Printed in the United States of America

1. 9 8 7 6 5 4 3 2 1

Contents

FAMILY TREE

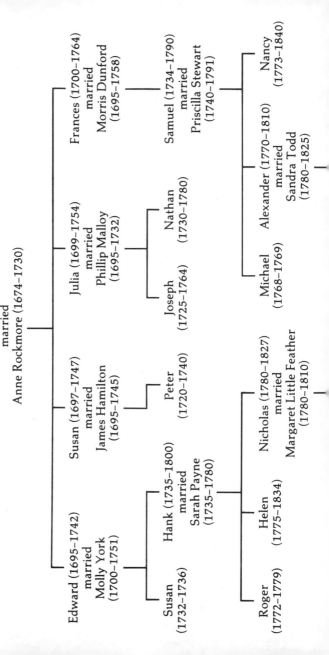

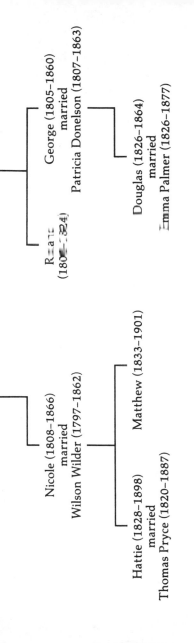

George (1805–1860)
married
Patricia Donelson (1807–1863)

R__a__ __
(180__–__824)

Douglas (1826–1864)
married
Emma Palmer (1826–1877)

Nicole (1808–1866)
married
Wilson Wilder (1797–1862)

Matthew (1833–1901)

Hattie (1828–1898)
married
Thomas Pryce (1820–1887)

AN AMERICAN FAMILY™ SERIES

FORTUNE IN MEN'S EYES

CHAPTER 1

Separation

On the night of August 21, 1853, Matthew Wilder threw a little party for himself—out on the trail. He lit a cheerful campfire, ate a meal of beans and corn, and sang a song to his horse.

It was a night he didn't want to forget. Not because any great event of man or nature had taken place. No, this was much more personal. He felt good about surviving three whole weeks away from his parents. And he wasn't even homesick.

It was a cause for celebration. A landmark of his own independence. The fire seemed brighter and warmer than any he had ever lit. The meal seemed tastier than any he had prepared before it. And the song . . . well, his horse didn't seem to mind it any.

The stars he could see in the Western sky that night numbered in the millions. Matthew lay awake for an hour, counting nearly 80 shooting stars. He figured he was a very lucky young man.

Matthew thought back to all the people he had come across in the past three weeks. His father told him he would not meet a soul. He'd said that if the wolves didn't get him the loneliness and boredom would. But it was not like that—not like that at all. The borderless highways of the plains that would one day be Colorado and Wyoming were alive with travelers. Many of them were just like himself. But there were also fortune hunters, runaways, prospectors, trappers, and Indian scouts.

The travelers told of fortunes won and lost. Of gold and silver running like rivers that are just out of reach. But all the woe, misery and failure in their adventures did not worry Matthew Wilder.

Most of the storytellers showed signs of being drunkards, or weak fools wanting only a good time. He was different.

If there was any gold to find, he knew he would find it. He'd stake his claim and reap the rewards. He would ride back into town a hero, a rich hero at that. And his father, mother, and all his friends would take notice. No, he was not worried about defeat. If anything, the prospectors' mistakes served as lessons.

All together it had been a grand three weeks. The days may have been hot and long. And at times the ride was tiring and the trail rough. But he was on his own. And the world was opening up before him. The west itself seemed to be welcoming him. The voices in the wind seemed to sing, "Take my hills and valleys, my rivers and my gold. They have been waiting since the dawn of time . . . just for you." And on this night, the world *was* Matthew Wilder's, and he cherished it.

Matthew thought back to the days just before he had left home. Compared to the way he felt now, those days seemed like a bad dream. They were filled with pain and sorrow, goodbyes and heartaches.

He remembered that it had been a warm summer day when he and his sister Hattie had said goodbye. But it was Hattie who was leaving that day—not Matthew.

They had set out on a picnic, under the oak tree down by the stream. Just Hattie and Matthew and their dog, Wigwam. Hattie had made a plateful of fried chicken and they'd brought along some lemonade. Hattie had to keep Wigwam from making grabs at the chicken. Matthew could still hear her voice:

"No, Wigwam. Git," she snapped at the naughty mutt. "That dog! It was you who taught him to beg and steal from the table, Matthew," Hattie said. But Matthew wasn't listening to his sister. He was staring back toward their house. Hattie took note of his daydream.

"Matthew? Are you okay?" she asked him.

"I don't want you leaving," Matthew said. "I don't know why you have to do this."

"Because I'm getting married, silly," she said.

"You have lots of men who want to marry you right here in town," Matthew said. "Why do you have to go marry some man from South Carolina?"

"You know I have to get away from here, Matthew," she said.

"You don't love us. Me, Mamma, or Pa."

"That's not true and you know it," Hattie answered. She shook him and made him look her in the eye. "I'm not trying to run away from you. I *love* my family. I'll miss you more than a coyote misses a full moon. But Thomas is a wealthy man. He owns a business back east. He's well respected. Everyone knows him. This is my chance to have all the things I've ever read or heard about."

"Do you love him?" Matthew asked.

"Oh, it's not all that simple," she told her brother. "You'll understand when you're a little older. There's more to marrying than just love. You have to respect the person. You should admire what he does and what he stands for, too."

"Well . . ." Matthew said. "It wouldn't hurt to like him a little, too. You've done a lot of talking about Mr. Thomas Pryce of South Carolina. But with all your talk, you haven't ever once mentioned liking him. I may only be 20 years old, but I know that much. I surely do."

"Oh that's enough, Matthew," Hattie said and turned away. "Let's just eat and stop all this talking. I worked like a mule making this picnic for us. Let's just have a good time."

So they decided not to talk anymore about Thomas Pryce or South Carolina. Matthew crunched down hard on the chicken, as though he were gobbling up all his fears and anger.

After a few minutes he almost forgot that in two hours Hattie would be gone—maybe forever. When would he ever get to travel back east to see his sister? The East held no charm or mystery for Matthew. Hattie had always dreamed of the fine life in a big city. Matthew dreamed of mountains, wide open spaces, and gold. This was why he decided to head west as soon as he could. He'd leave Hatfield's Bluff soon after Hattie did.

Their time at the picnic flew by. Soon the sun began to sink lower in the western sky.

"Lordy!" Hattie suddenly yelled, scaring the dog. "Look at the sun. Why it must be close to four."

Sure enough, almost as soon as Hattie said those words, the church bells struck four o'clock. The bells only rang twice a week: on Sundays for worship, and later at four, when the weekly stage heading east was set to leave town.

"Hurry Matthew. Grab what you can. Just scoop everything up. Hurry. I'll be late. I'll miss the stage," she cried.

"Wouldn't that be too bad."

"Matthew Wilder, don't sass me. If I miss that stage, I'll . . ."

Before Matthew could gather up the chicken, his sister was running down the road toward town. Wigwam followed quickly on her trail.

"Hattie, wait!" Matthew cried.

"Hurry!" she cried as she and the dog disappeared around the bend.

Matthew left the rest of the chicken for the birds. He just tucked the basket under his arm and hustled toward town as best he could.

When he arrived, his mother and father were already there. They were standing by the stage, hugging and fussing over Hattie. Matthew could not help but notice that Thomas Pryce stood by, tall and erect. He seemed almost proud that he was taking Hattie away.

"We gotta move out," the stage driver yelled. The man scrambled to his place and took the reins of the six-horse team.

"Hattie!" Matthew cried out and waved. He dropped the basket and raced as fast as he could to her side. He gave her one last hug.

"Take care of yourself," Matthew said.

Then with a little more command in his voice he addressed Mr. Thomas Pryce. "You take care of her, too."

"That I will, son," came the gentleman's reply.

"Oh, Matthew," Hattie said, hugging her brother again, long and hard. "I'll be fine. You know I'll be fine. I'll be with family. Well, almost family," she added.

Thomas Pryce was a business partner of the Dunfords, Matthew and Hattie's cousins. But that was of little comfort to Matthew. He knew little about these cousins. He had never met the Dunfords and didn't care to.

Finally Hattie let go of Matthew and stood tall. But there were tears in her eyes. "My. I don't know when I've had so much fussing done over me," she said. "I'll try to make it last." And in what seemed like a second, Hattie Wilder was gone.

Matthew could still hear her words floating along the night wind. It hurt him to think about Hattie. The passing weeks had not lessened his sadness. How could his sister have gone off with that businessman from South Carolina? He wondered where she was tonight. He wondered how her journey was coming. Was she home yet? Was she happy? He might never know.

Finally the deep sorrow of his thoughts gave way to the more powerful urge for sleep. He drifted off looking forward to another adventuresome day on the trail. But when he woke at dawn, it was not the bright morning sun that first greeted him. Nor was it the crystal blue sky. Matthew awoke to a shotgun aimed right between his eyes.

The Quiet Stranger

At the other end of the gun stood a tall, muscular black man. Matthew could not clearly make out his face. The sun was behind the man, casting a dark shadow over his brow. He wore a wide brimmed hat set low on his forehead. The man said nothing, but waited for Matthew to get up.

This is not how Matthew wanted to begin his day. And certainly not how he wanted to end it. "Morning," he finally said meekly.

The black man said nothing.

Matthew cautiously rose to his elbows. "Coffee?" he asked.

The black man nodded. But he kept the gun right between Matthew's eyes.

"I'll need to get up in order to make it, you know?" Matthew said.

The black man took a cautious step back as Matthew stood and stretched. Since the beginning of his journey, Matthew had met lots of men with guns. He felt it didn't pay to be scared of them. The men could read your fears and take advantage of them. "Help me get this fire going," Matthew said. But the black man hesitated. "Look. I don't mind sharing what I have with you," Matthew said firmly. "But you're going to have to help, or you can just git."

The black man, surprised at the show of courage, let the gun drop to his side.

"That's better," said Matthew. And for the first time, he got a good look at the man. He seemed to be about ten years older than Matthew. He was dirty and tired, and his clothes didn't fit well. There were holes in his buckskin shirt and his boots were shoddy and worn.

Matthew began to wonder if the man was an outlaw. He had the same wild look in his eyes that Matthew had seen in so many other travelers. But in the others he also saw fear. In this man he saw no fear. The black man's eyes were calm. Or maybe they were just empty—lacking any feeling or emotion.

"What's your name, friend?" Matthew asked. When he didn't get an answer, he went on. "Mine's Wilder. Matthew Wilder. People call me Matt."

The black man finally set his gun beside a stone and threw some wood into a pile. "The name's Zeke," the man said in a grave whisper.

"Zeke what?"

"Just Zeke."

All right, Matthew thought. If he wants to be that way, let him. I don't need company.

After a few moments, Matthew got the fire going and brewed up some coffee. The two men sat in silence for about a half an hour, slowly drinking their coffee.

Finally Matthew gathered up his few possessions and started to saddle up. Zeke looked up at him. But he didn't move an inch from his spot by the fire.

"I'm heading for the trail," Matthew said in a stiff voice. "You're welcome to ride along. Or you can stay here. It's all the same to me."

Zeke slowly got up. He threw the rest of his coffee away, and put out the fire. Then he saddled up, too, and turned his horse around.

"Guess I'll ride along for a spell," he finally said. "You seem harmless—and you ain't so curious as to be annoying."

In anger Matthew started to say something, but then changed his mind. Instead he spurred his horse forward, and mumbled, "Suit yourself."

The two men rode side by side without a word for several miles. Finally Matthew decided to make one more effort to get Zeke to open up. Then he'd quit trying—and ride off on his own at the first opportunity.

"Where you headed?" Matthew asked. "California's my spot. That's where I'm going. Near as I figure, another day's ride and I should join up with a wagon train at Miller's Ridge. That suits me fine. Past Miller's Ridge it's Indian territory. You don't want to ride alone through there."

Matthew was hoping his own enthusiasm might loosen Zeke's tongue. "Plan to find gold in California. People have been getting rich for years there. Now it's my turn."

But the more Matthew talked, the more he realized what he had suspected for some time. It wasn't common to see a black man riding by himself in the Colorado Territory. And one that looked like Zeke was probably running from something.

"You been riding by yourself for a long time?" Matthew asked.

"A ways."

"You must have passed through Indian country."

"Yeah. Some. They don't seem to mind seeing a black man. Not as afraid of a black man as they are of white men."

"You're right there," Matthew replied. "My pa was a trapper. Used to trade with Indians. But they liked him. My mamma was half Indian, too. That makes me part Indian, you know."

Matthew continued to talk, trying to make conversation with the man riding beside him. But the more Matthew looked into Zeke's eyes, the more he realized the truth.

"You're a runaway, aren't you?" Matthew said at last. Zeke said nothing. But for the first time since he'd met him, Matthew saw fear in Zeke's eyes. What was strangely missing before now seemed to be written all over his face.

"You're a slave," Matthew said. He even surprised himself as he heard the words escape his lips. "A runaway."

Zeke suddenly stopped his horse in its tracks. He looked at Matthew with a fierce gaze. "I am," he said simply.

Matthew knew about runaway slaves, though he had never seen one before. He couldn't remember hearing of anyone making it out this far. Of course he had seen plenty of other black men before. Old Jake Granger had some negro help ranching his lands. Matthew had never thought of them as slaves though. And it didn't cross his mind now to take advantage of Zeke's situation.

"I don't aim to make trouble for you, friend," said Matthew.

"I got a price on my head," Zeke replied. It was almost as if he were taunting him to try something. "Five hundred dollars."

"Ha," said Matthew. "I'll make that much in my first month prospecting." But as he thought about it, the price seemed quite high for an ordinary slave.

"That's a lot of money for a slave," said Matthew.

"Yep," said Zeke. Then he tugged on the reins and clicked his horse forward. "But the price is just about right to put on the head of a *murderer*."

Zeke's Story

Matthew was truly frightened for the first time since he'd left home. Here he was, in the middle of nowhere, riding with a murderer. After Zeke had made that statement, he had said nothing. He simply rode on, as though the matter was closed. Matthew thought it best not to bring it up again. But he watched Zeke with a new found suspicion. He also unlatched the strap that held his six-shooter in place.

It was not until supper time that the two men spoke about it again.

"I'm hungry," Zeke finally said.

"Well," Matthew began, "I got enough food to last one person till Miller's Ridge. I don't know how much farther you plan on riding along. But if it's all the way there, you best figure out some way to help feed us. I'm not your mess tent, you know."

Zeke stopped his horse and stared at Matthew. Immediately, Matthew's blood ran cold. Who had Matthew thought he was talking to—an old friend? This was a man who said he was a murderer! Matthew thought of several ways of apologizing. But before he could voice a single one, Zeke took off like a bolt of lightning.

"Hey!" Matthew cried. "Wait." But Zeke could not hear past the thundering of his horse's hooves. He was heading for a grove of trees about a mile away.

Matthew did not know what to do. Would Zeke be back? Had he really run off, angered or somehow hurt by what Matthew had said? Matthew couldn't make up his mind whether to ride off or follow Zeke. So he chose the middle ground. He found a cluster of rocks and decided to wait in what little shade they cast.

"I'll give him half an hour to get himself back here," he announced. "Then he can ride the wind for all I care."

A few moments later, Matthew heard a gunshot. He stood to see if he could make out the direction of the sound. As he did, he saw Zeke racing back toward him. When Zeke's horse got closer, Matthew saw there was an animal strapped to its back. He shielded his eyes against the light of the bright sun. As he did, he saw a huge jack rabbit drop. It landed at his feet.

"That do it?" asked Zeke. He dismounted and started to gather firewood. "You ever skin a rabbit?"

"Sure."

"Well, you'd better get to it. I'll be done with the fire in no time." Without another word, Zeke began building their fire for the night.

"I'm sorry Zeke," Matthew said. "I just meant that you needed to help—"

"That's what I've done, haven't I? You told me to jump, and I jumped."

Matthew thought it best to leave well enough alone. The two men worked at their chores for awhile. Finally Zeke looked up at Matthew. "Why did your family let you go off into country like this?" he asked.

"Oh, well, my mamma and pa didn't have much say in this. Sometimes a man has to set off to see things for himself. And it's no one else's business, is it?"

Zeke laughed. "You ran away, too, didn't you?"

Matthew looked truly hurt. "What?"

"No father or mother lets a son just up and drift away when he feels it's time. Especially the kind of folks the son still calls mamma and pa."

"I told them of my plans," Matthew said.

"I reckon that's true," Zeke said. "You told them you had some big ideas to go off and conquer the world. But I vow you didn't tell them *when* you were doing all this. Nope. One night you were there, and the next you were gone. And half the kitchen stock with you."

Matthew hated to have the truth held up to him so boldly. He had just spent three weeks telling himself that his folks must have known it was coming. Now suddenly it all seemed like a big lie. He *had* run away from home. He had left without a single goodbye. And just as quickly as the truth fell on him, Matthew felt homesick.

Zeke asked, "Why'd you do it?"

"I don't know."

"Don't you?"

"My sister left home. She got married, moved back east. After that, I guess I just felt like there was nothing left for me. Me and Hattie used to be real close. As long as she was around, I didn't have to think about my life. With her gone, everything just seemed like chores. My pa's a tracker, a trader. He deals in furs, pelts, things like that. I helped him out."

"Won't he miss you?" asked Zeke.

"Nah. My pa always said that Hattie had a better head for business. That's the truth. She's smart as a whip. Me . . . I just always abided it. I put in my time helping my pa, but I didn't have much heart for it. He'll get along fine without me.

"Anyway," Matthew continued, "there wasn't much reason to hang around anymore. But I'll be back someday. Then I'll buy the town I grew up in and everything in it. And then I can give my mamma a rest. She's lived a dozen lives all rolled into one, I swear I'll go back, Zeke, you'll see."

Zeke just said, "I believe you boy. I do believe you."

"How about you?" Matthew asked.

"Me?"

"Yeah. I mean, why did *you* run? Did they beat you? I'll bet I know. I bet somebody whipped you. And you hit him back and accidentally killed him, right?"

Zeke watched the fire catch and the flames leap through the dead wood. He thought about telling Matthew a lie. Just to keep the young man from asking anymore questions. But the truth of it was, Zeke wanted to get it off his chest. Lord knows he had no one else to tell. No one else had even bothered to ask.

"It ain't the beating. You can take that," he said. "You hurt, you bleed. But the bleeding stops. The hurt goes away. God built men to take it. And it's not the food—the stuff you wouldn't feed your pigs—you get used to it. You even thank the Lord for it. It keeps you going. And it's not being cussed out or laughed at either. All that you can take. It's none of that. But it's something else just as real, but harder to say.

"At first you're fine. There's this little voice inside you that tells you how good you are. Even when everyone else cusses you. When life seems bad today, the little voice says things will be better tomorrow. It tells you to sing when you feel like crying. It tells you to turn away when you feel like fighting back.

"But then something happens. You wake up one morning and you notice the little voice isn't there anymore. And you get real quiet. You listen for it, but it's gone. You work and you can't sing. You hurt, and you don't feel better. You get hit, and you want to hit back. Because the voice inside you is missing. And when that happens, you start to disappear.

"So I ran away all right. I ran away to try to find myself and that little voice inside me. It's out there somewhere. It just got lost, buried like your gold. But I aim to dig it up. And then maybe I can ride back into *my* town someday. If I can, I'll be richer than any man alive."

Matthew could not look at Zeke. He just stared into the fire. He wondered what it was like to be a slave. He tried to imagine it. But he couldn't do it.

Matthew had never had a savage beating. He'd never lost that little voice inside. Matthew knew what Zeke meant about that. He had a little voice inside him, too. But his voice was different from the one Zeke had, he was sure. For Matthew, the little voice was what was pushing him to California to find gold. For Zeke, the little voice was what had kept him alive. It was a space between them that could never be bridged by any talk. And yet, somehow, Matthew felt a closeness to this stranger.

They cooked the rabbit and ate it heartily. It was tough, but it tasted good. Later, Matthew and Zeke sat before the fire and listened to some poor coyote crying to the rising moon.

Matthew felt at ease once more, as though things would be all right. He hoped Zeke would ride on with him toward Miller's Ridge. But there was still a matter that kept eating away at Matthew. And it kept him from truly trusting the man who sat across from the leaping flames.

"Zeke?"

"Yeah."

"Who did you kill?"

Zeke looked across at the youth. He frowned and said, "Don't look for trouble."

"I have to know," Matthew replied.

"It's best you just leave it be. It's best you don't know. And it's best you ride along without me tomorrow."

"You don't have to ride on alone," Matthew said. "There's Indian country up ahead. You'll need the safety of the wagon train same as me."

"I made it this far," Zeke said. He looked at Matthew's face. He could see it was still filled with questions. Zeke sighed. He picked up a stick and played with it. He was trying to decide how and where to begin. "It was an accident," he said finally.

Matthew seemed relieved and almost laughed out loud. "I *knew* it was an accident. I knew you couldn't kill a man on purpose."

"Yeah, well . . . it was an accident, like I said. There are some people back east, they help slaves to escape."

"Who are these people?" Matthew asked.

"People same as you and me. Black and white who think all folks should be free. There are more of them than you might think. But they've got to work in secret, because some states still make it legal to own slaves.

"I was in Missouri," Zeke continued. "They moved me from house to house, mile after mile—mostly at night. I was supposed to meet up with a family who'd take me in for good. But as a *free* man. Then, it happened . . ."

"What happened Zeke? Tell me." Matthew urged him.

"The Harlan brothers. Jeb and Hank. They're like your pa in a way. They hunt—but they hunt for men. They trap and kill them, just like animals. The Harlans found out about the route I took. One night they cornered me in a barn. Hank aimed his gun right at me and fired."

"Did he hit you?"

"The gun backfired. He killed himself, plain and simple. Everyone knew it, too, even Jeb. I ran and hid in an old shack that night. But the next day I heard two men saying that I was the one who killed Hank. The town put a price on my head, and Jeb was coming to get me. I've been on the run ever since. He's no more than a day's ride behind me. So I can't stay with you. If he gets to me there's no telling what he'll do to you."

"I'm not scared," Matthew declared. "Besides, there's two of us Zeke. Harlan doesn't stand a chance. You're strong, and you must have a good aim to bag this hare with one shot. And I'm the sharpest shooter this side of Miller's Ridge."

Matthew's hearty courage almost made Zeke laugh. "If you had any sense, you'd try to take me in yourself."

"Heck," said Matthew. "If I had any sense, I would have stayed in Hatfield's Bluff with my mamma and pa."

Both Zeke and Matthew began to laugh. They laughed long, hard, and loud. It felt good to laugh. A short time later, the two men drifted off to sleep.

It wasn't until dawn that their sleep was interrupted. As an orange glow began to form in the eastern sky, they heard the sound of thunder. It was faint, distant thunder. But it suddenly put fear into their hearts.

Zeke and Matthew looked up to the sky. It was free of clouds, and promised as fine a sunrise as anyone could ask for.

"Can't be a storm on the way," Zeke said.

"Shhh," Matthew said.

"What?"

"Listen."

The two men grew quiet. The thunder grew louder and louder by the moment. Both men realized at the same instant that this was the thunder of animals.

"Buffalo?" Zeke said.

"Too fast, too light," Matthew said. He put his ear to the ground. "Horses," he said. As soon as he said it, they saw a cloud of dust on the horizon.

"Wild horses?" asked Zeke.

"Not enough of them. From the dust, I reckon there's no more than a dozen."

Zeke peered through the gray of the morning. "Riders. I see riders. Indians?"

"Not Indians," Matthew said confidently. "I've seen Indians ride. They don't make that kind of racket. They ride soft. And they don't stir up the dust like that. Look—"

Both men could just make out the approaching forms. The solid mass began to break up into individual parts. There seemed to be about ten riders. One of them was carrying a red, white, and blue flag. Whoever they were, they were riding as if the very devil was chasing them.

"They're government," Matthew said.

As the group came closer, Matthew could see that they were all in uniform, except for one. He appeard to be an Indian scout. One of the men was strapped face down across his saddle. His horse was tied to the horse of another. Matthew saw that the riders were led by an officer, probably a captain, going by his dress.

In another instant the band of men bore down on Matthew and Zeke. All the horses came to a halt behind the captain. He was a dark man, with a big mustache and long black hair. The dust and dirt could hide neither the fear nor the rage in his eyes. He calmed his horse as best he could and took a swift look behind him.

"Good morning, sir," Matthew said.

"No time for introductions or pleasantries, son," the captain answered. He glanced quickly around the small camp Matthew and

Zeke had made. "Looks like there's just the two of you here."

"That's right," Matthew said. "Is anything wrong?"

"As wrong as wrong can be," the captain answered. "You two better come with us. Hit your mounts and ride if you value your lives. We just left an Indian settlement. Seven of my men are back there, face down in the dirt with arrows in their backs."

The Captain's Plan

Matthew looked around at the other men. Half of them were bloody and wounded. There were wild looks in their eyes. Even the scout, called Yellow Cloud by the captain, seemed dazed and shaken.

"I won't repeat myself, gentlemen," the captain told Matthew and Zeke. Then he bellowed to his troops, "Hang and rattle, men. Hoaa." The men took off as swiftly as they had arrived.

"Think the Indians will come?" asked Zeke.

"I don't want to find out," Matthew answered. "Let's follow them."

33

Matthew quickly mounted his horse. But Zeke held back. "What's the matter?" Matthew asked. Zeke just stared at Matthew, a worried look on his face.

"Come on Zeke. You want to wind up like those soldiers, with an arrow in your back?"

"I can't go," Zeke said.

It dawned on Matthew why Zeke was so afraid. If the soldiers were to learn about Zeke's past, they might arrest him and send him back. But Matthew refused to believe the worst. He figured the soldiers would not be bothered with the problems of the South. They had their own problems—namely the Indians.

"Well, I'm not leaving you here," Matthew said. "As far as they're concerned, you and I set out on our own. You're a ranch hand who worked for my family, all right? Now let's get out of here."

It was a hard six miles to the military camp. At the foot of a hill, Matthew counted about a dozen tents. This was no army. It was just a small garrison of no more than two dozen men.

After they reached camp, Matthew and Zeke settled into a spare tent. They rinsed themselves off with water from a tin pitcher and bowl. Then Zeke sat very still, dog tired from the ride. He stared down at the bare earth beneath him. Matthew knew he was still afraid of being found out. The two men sat in their tent, wondering what would happen next.

Matthew looked over at Zeke. He had his shirt off, a towel draped across his neck. And for the first time, Matthew saw it. On Zeke's left shoulder, barely visible, was a series of small raised bumps. At first Matthew could not figure out what it was. A scar, yes. But from what?

Then he looked more closely. And he saw that the letter "X" had been burned into Zeke's skin. He had been branded, Matthew realized, like a steer. In their brief time together, Matthew had looked upon Zeke as strong and fearless. But now, sitting there, half naked and crouched near the ground, the black man looked different. He seemed small, weak, and full of fear.

Matthew wanted to tell him how sorry he was. He wanted to let Zeke know that he didn't think less of him as a man. He certainly didn't think of Zeke as a "thing" that could be "owned" by another person. If anything, Zeke deserved all the respect in the world for having gone through what he had.

Just as Matthew opened his mouth to speak, the tent flap flew open. Zeke hurriedly threw his shirt over his chest to cover the mark on his shoulder.

"Men?" It was Captain Grade. He had gotten cleaned up and seemed rested now. The fear in his eyes was replaced by a grim determination. "You two men all right?"

"Yes," Matthew said. "Are you?"

The captain was surprised at the question. He showed a slight smile. "Yes, young man, I'll be all right. As soon as I tack a few Indian hides to my tent."

"Just what happened back there?" asked Matthew.

"A while back we made a treaty with the Apaches," the captain said. "Gave them 6600 acres of land around here, far more than they needed. We've had a lot of settlers come out here. But I don't know any good reason why we can't share this land. That's all we want to do, share the land.

"My orders were to resettle some of the savages. Allow for all of us to have a piece of God's earth. But let me tell you, the Apaches have a different idea of fairness, son. You could fit the entire tribe in 600 acres with room to spare. But they want it all. There's a hot-blooded batch of them, about 100, who won't budge."

"Isn't it their land though?" Matthew said innocently. He realized too late that his remark would probably anger the captain. And it did.

"It's *our* land, son. We gave it to them. Hear what I'm saying? Gave them scot-free what it would cost a white man dearly for. *We* aim to *use* this land, do something with it. We want to use it as it was meant to be used. But the savages just sit on it. They're too lazy to do anything but hunt and drink on it."

"So the government wants the land back?" asked Matthew.

"Not really. The aim is to move them to another stretch of land. It's a bit smaller, but just as pretty. And it's just as good for their needs. They wouldn't lose a thing. But you just try telling the Apaches that. They're a thickheaded bunch."

As soon as those words left the captain's lips, he suddenly stared at Matthew. He stared at him long and hard. It was as if he were seeing him for the first time. It dawned on Matthew why. Though Matthew's features were white like his father's, he had his mother's dark, brick-red skin. Usually it was not very noticeable. But now, after weeks under the harsh plains sun, it shone a bright red.

The captain looked both sheepish and a little annoyed at once. "Of course not all Indians are bad, mind you. My Indian scout, Yellow Cloud, is as true and as good a man as they come. I'm not like some. I don't hate just for the sake of hating. But when seven good men get murdered for no earthly reason, I get mad!"

"What are you going to do?" The timid voice came from Zeke, who had remained quiet until then.

"There's no way for a handful of men to roust a hundred Apaches. I sent a rider on ahead to get help. There will be another 100 men here by next week. In the meantime, I don't plan to sit by while the bodies of my men lie rotting on the open plain. Tomorrow we ride back and take an eye for an eye. Just like the Bible says. My men need to get their guts and spirit back. And they will if we take seven Indians to their graves.

"You two are safe here. After the attack we'll ride on to meet the reinforcements. We can deposit both of you on a wagon train, safe out of Indian country. That's all. There's food in the mess tent. Make yourselves at home."

He walked out, leaving Matthew disturbed and frightened. "He's talking about murder, plain and simple."

"I suppose so," Zeke said. "But what do you call what the Indians did?"

"They're trying to protect what little they got left. My pa told me about these treaties the government signs and then backs out of. Happens all the time. Give the red man some land, then take it away. Till finally there's nothing left. The captain ought to know better."

"Well," said Zeke. "I guess he's got no choice."

"What?"

"He's got a bunch of angry, defeated men on his hands. They want revenge."

"How can *you* of all people say that?" Matthew asked. "How can you just sit there and—"

"Because I know what it feels like to want revenge. I also know that getting angry and upset about it won't change a thing. Those soldiers plan on doing some killing. They're going to do it, with or without our approval. And another thing. I'm not about to say 'boo' to that captain. I've come hundreds of miles to get this far, to be as free as I'll ever be. I won't do *anything* to risk that."

Zeke stormed out of the tent. Matthew suddenly felt alone and out of control. Things were happening too fast. "It just isn't fair," he said to himself. "It's not right to move Indians off one piece of land and put them on another. Not just so whites and Indians can 'share' the land? What gave white people the right to tell the Indians where to live."

Matthew laid down on his wool blanket and started to doze off. He slept for a few minutes, but was soon awakened by the sound of Zeke's voice. Matthew actually sat up, thinking that Zeke was talking to him. But then he realized that Zeke was still outside the tent. He was talking to someone else. Matthew listened carefully, for he heard fear in Zeke's voice. He soon understood why. Zeke was being addressed by Captain Grade.

"Hello Zeke. You and the boy have everything you need?"

"Yes sir, we're fine."

"Good. Say, I don't believe you said where you were from."

"Well, uh . . ." Zeke stammered.

"You don't hail from Missouri, do you?"

"Missouri?"

"Yeah. A few days ago I ran into a fella comes from Missouri," the captain said. "A white man." The captain paused for a moment. Zeke remained silent. Matthew could almost feel the man's fear from the other side of the tent.

"This fella was pretty angry," the captain said. "He told me he was looking for someone. He said some negro fella ran away from his owner and killed this man's brother. Yep, a negro, that's what he said."

Matthew froze in horror. The captain knew about Zeke! What would he do? Matthew sat inside the tent straining to hear every word.

The captain went on. "Now what do you suppose the odds are of there being two negroes running around these parts? One being the object of this white man's hunt.

And the other just being some innocent wanderer."

"It would be possible, I guess," said Zeke.

"Think so?" the Captain asked. "Maybe you're right. Still, I wonder if both of these negroes—the innocent and the murderer— would have a brand on them. The kind of brand they give slaves. That would put two negro slaves right smack in the middle of the same five-mile area." The captain paused a moment before adding, "Now *that* doesn't seem very possible, does it? Now let's see if I can recall this white man's name. Jud? No, ah, Jeb. That's right. Jeb Harlan. Wore a buckskin coat."

"Please sir," said Zeke. "Please . . ." but that was all Zeke could manage.

It was all Matthew could stand. He could no longer sit by while the Captain had his merciless fun with Zeke. He burst out of the tent and found himself in between the two large men.

"Now hold on Captain," said Matthew. "Zeke is my pa's ranch hand. Him and me set out together to find our riches, stake a claim. I don't know who's been telling you stories about runaway slaves but—"

Zeke cut Matthew short. "It's no use," he said. "The captain here knows. That man Jeb, he'll be chasing me for the rest of my days. I guess I'd tire sooner or later anyway. No one can keep running forever."

"Better leave this to me son," said the captain.

"What are you going to do to him?" demanded Matthew. "He hasn't done anything wrong. He didn't kill that man. It was an accident."

The captain put up his hands in protest to stop Matthew. "Now hold on there, my boy. As I figure it, this has nothing to do with you."

Matthew ignored the captain's warning. "You try to turn this man in . . ." Matthew paused to gather his courage. He knew he was about to say something he would regret. But he could not stop the words. They seemed to have a life of their own. ". . . I'll stop you any way I can!"

"Matthew, shut up," Zeke said.

Matthew tried his best to look fierce. But it wasn't something he was suited for. He was a little put off when he saw a smile come over the captain's face. "I believe you would try to stop me," the captain said. "But I don't think things need to come to that."

Then Captain Grade turned to Zeke. "I don't have any wish to put you in chains," he told him. "As far as this murder goes, I guess you could be just as innocent as you could be guilty. But I'm sworn to uphold the law. Now that man, Jeb, is no more than a day's ride from here. I can either give you to him, or tell him to ride on."

Matthew knew the captain was getting at something. He knew Zeke would be asked to do something in return for Grade's silence.

"I believe a man has to earn his freedom," the captain said. "That's especially true out west. I can promise you freedom. But I need your help with our raid on the Indians."

"Don't do it," Matthew said.

"Hush," Zeke commanded. "Captain? If you can make good on your promise, I'll do whatever you ask."

"What are you saying Zeke?" Matthew cried.

But Zeke did not answer. He just lowered his head and turned away from Matthew.

The captain, however, looked Matthew right in the eye. "It appears, son, that you have some growing yet to do. If you call this man your friend, you'll get back to your tent and let us talk in private."

Matthew looked on in silence, drowning in his own confusion. He watched Captain Grade lead Zeke away by the shoulder. The two men disappeared into the captain's tent.

Escape

Matthew went back into his tent and dropped down onto the wool blanket. He felt lonely and frustrated. He wished he had never left home. He wished he was still helping his father with the furs. Or better yet, he wished his sister had never left home at all. Why couldn't life be just like it was before Hattie left?

It was nearing dusk before Zeke finally came back. Matthew had grabbed some beans and bread from a cranky cook earlier and brought them back to his tent. He was finishing the food when Zeke closed the tent flap behind him.

The big black man said nothing. He sat down across from Matthew and played absently with a twig.

Matthew looked up, held out his plate of food and said, "Want some?"

Zeke said. "No. I ate with the captain."

"I figured you might have," Matthew said quietly. "What did he ask you to do?"

"It's probably best you don't know," said Zeke.

"I want to know."

"He wants me to go with the men on the raid tomorrow night."

"And do what?"

Zeke hesitated. Then he finally said, "The Indians here don't see too many black men. They tend to think black men have magical powers, that they're signs of good fortune. The captain thinks that the Apache leaders would be the most curious. And if I was to appear in their camp as a magic man, well, I could lead them to a nearby creek, then . . ."

Zeke couldn't get the rest of the story out. But Matthew knew what came next. He said

". . . then the captain and his men open fire from behind the rocks and trees and bushes. And they cut down the tribe's leaders just like that. Just like they were hunting buffalo. Just like they were killing a bunch of animals. I swear, Zeke, you did more than eat with the captain. You sold your soul to—"

"Shut up!" cried Zeke. "I've listened to your bellyaching long enough. You moan on and on about the Indians. You don't like it? Then *you do* something about it. You go off and live with them. Fight and die with them, too. But don't talk to me about selling my soul. No sir. I'm getting my soul *back*. That's what I'm doing. I'm gettin' it back!"

He stood and kicked the dirt in anger. Matthew tensed and backed away. Zeke said, "Look around you boy. You can't help but see all sorts of suffering and misery. Black people surely have their share, and so do the Indians. But so do the thousands of white folks who come pouring into the west like locusts. Babies die, cattle die, folks get killed or maybe kill others. It goes on and on all the time. Just cause you finally sit up and take notice doesn't mean it's going to stop. No sir. But I'm gonna do something about it—for me.

"I've had enough misery for a whole tribe of Indians and then some," Zeke went on. "One more day of hell, one more day of shame isn't going to kill me. Tomorrow night I'm going to be free once and for all. When you get an 'X' like the one on my shoulder, then you can preach to me. Till that day, leave me alone! Got that? Now if you don't like it, get out. Go to California and make your fortune. Git!"

Zeke stormed out of the tent. Matthew felt small and childlike. It was as though he had been scolded by his father. Matthew hated himself because he felt like crying. He wanted to show Zeke that he was a real man. He wanted to show he was as bold and as wise as any man. Instead, he felt like a bowl of jelly inside. He felt like some prissy school-girl, soft and weak. He heard Zeke's stinging words over and over again in his head— "Leave me alone . . . leave me alone."

Matthew finally fell asleep. When he awoke in the middle of the night, he heard Zeke snoring nearby. The man had returned to the tent so quietly that Matthew hadn't heard a sound. Zeke had simply put his head down and slept.

Matthew looked over at the black man. Matthew knew that Zeke must have had just as tough a night as he had. In less than 24 hours, Zeke would lead the captain's soldiers on their raid. The hunted had turned into the hunter.

Matthew realized for the first time that life held no easy answers. It would be a struggle from now on. For himself as well as for Zeke. He hoped that Zeke would be free by tomorrow. He hoped that the white men and the Indians could indeed "share" the land. But whatever happened, Matthew knew that he could not stay another minute in that camp. He could not be a party to the killing that was about to take place.

He would leave tonight. Before dawn. He would leave Zeke and the captain and continue his journey west. He'd head straight for California, to the gold, to seek his fortune. And maybe in a little while, all this would seem like nothing more than a bad dream.

Matthew slept restlessly for the next two hours. Then around four o'clock he got up and dressed quickly. Zeke was sound asleep. Matthew tiptoed over to the entrance of the tent. Then he looked back at the sleeping black man.

"Goodbye friend," Matthew whispered in a soft voice. He closed the tent flap behind him.

Outside, the night was chilly and unusually damp. Walking softly Matthew found it was easy to sneak past the one sentry. Matthew and Zeke's horses were tied a short distance away from the soldier's mounts. Matthew found his horse quickly. He stroked its head and mane gently to keep him quiet. He placed the saddle carefully on the horse's back.

Then, in one swift motion, he leapt upon the horse, grabbed the reins, and drove his boot deep into the beast's side. He raced out of camp like a tumbleweed in a thunderstorm.

Before the sentry knew what had happened, Matthew was already on his way.

Onward he rode into the night, into the west, into the future. And soon he felt nothing but the horse beneath him and the dust in his teeth.

In the dark he could not see the trail clearly. He could not see the groove of earth dug out by skillful hands. Had he seen the trap, he might have been able to guide his horse over or around it. Instead, Matthew and his horse were suddenly thrown head over hoof. They crashed to the ground in a dusty heap.

The world seemed to be spinning around in a wild circle. Matthew jumped up and reached for his six-shooter. But it was gone. He stumbled around in the dirt, trying to find it. What was going on? Everything seemed to be happening in a feverish dream.

It was the knife that jolted him back to reality. The cold steel pressing into the fleshy part of his neck brought him to his senses.

"Who are you?" a voice growled. "Speak plain or die."

Matthew's Choice

Matthew felt a hand grab him by the chin and turn his head. In a flash, he was looking squarely into the eyes of an Indian. He had half expected to see war paint and a headdress of feathers. But instead of bright colors, paint, and beads, Matthew saw a plain face. It was as dark and as hard as a tombstone.

He tried to speak, but the Indian was choking him. Finally the man loosened his grip.

"My name is Matthew Wilder. I mean no harm."

"Did Grade send you?" the Indian asked in a deep, husky voice.

"What?"

"Captain Grade. Did he send you after me?"

"No."

The Indian tightened his grip, a warning to Matthew to speak the truth.

"I swear," said Matthew. "I ran out of the camp tonight."

"Why?"

"I was afraid. I didn't want to be a part of . . ." Matthew stopped short.

"A part of what?" the Indian demanded. He punctuated his sentence with a sharp jab of the knife handle.

"Aghh! Please!" Matthew cried.

"A part of the raid? Is that it?" the Indian asked. Matthew nodded his head once. "I thought so," the Indian said.

He spun Matthew around. Finally, by the light of the moon, Matthew got a better look at the Indian's face. It was Yellow Cloud—Captain Grade's own scout.

"Tell me what you know of the raid, Matthew Wilder."

"What? I can't do that."

"You must tell me. Many lives are at stake."

"Well, lives will be lost either way. Whether I tell you or not. Look. I don't want any part of this. That's why I left. They kill Indians, the Indians kill them. I just want to go to California and find my fortune."

"Your *fortune*, is that it?" Yellow Cloud said harshly. "Come on, my friend. Come with me and I'll show you some people's fortunes."

Matthew began to protest once more. But Yellow Cloud grabbed him by the neck and dragged him to his horse. He tied Matthew's horse to his own, threw Matthew atop his own mount and climbed up in front of him.

They rode through the night that way for several miles. Neither man said a word. Finally they arrived at a creek as dawn was breaking.

Matthew could hear the creek before he could clearly see it. The water babbled and gurgled as it flowed past rocks and fallen tree stumps. With a silver light now visible in the east, Matthew saw shapes taking form.

Yellow Cloud's ride had taken them up where the tree line began. Pines reached skyward. Rocks and bluffs peeked out here and there along the jagged horizon.

"There," said Yellow Cloud abruptly. He pointed to some large rocks that sat on the side of the creek bed. It took several minutes before Matthew's eyes adjusted to the light. But when he finally saw it, his blood turned cold. Before him was as strange a sight as he'd ever seen.

Matthew dismounted and walked toward the rocks. There, draped over the stones, were nearly a dozen pieces of clothing. Most of them were women's dresses made from the hides of buffaloes. But there were some smaller pieces too—children's clothing. All the clothes were heavily stained with blood.

Looking closer, Matthew could see that the dresses were ripped and cut. Several were shot through with bullet holes. One dress had no less than a dozen bullet holes in it.

Then he came upon the children's clothing. All were as bloody and manhandled as the adult's clothing. The sight could not have been more sickening to Matthew had the bodies themselves been in the clothes. Matthew turned around to ask Yellow Cloud about the clothes. He nearly jumped when he saw that the Indian was already standing behind him.

Yellow Cloud said, "They were doing their morning chores, washing their clothes, their hair. The children were playing in the creek. They watched the dawn, same as we do now. But it was not the sun they saw come up over the rim of the hill. It was some of Grade's men. The women and children were no more than targets for the soldiers. This was the 'fortune' of the women and children at Crow Creek. No gold, no silver, just a few moments of terror. Then the horrible silence of death."

Yellow Cloud knelt and touched the hem of one of the small dresses. "We leave the clothing to stain the rocks to remind the spirits of what happened here."

Matthew walked away, unable to take in the sight before him for another moment. Yellow Cloud rose and followed.

"So that's why the Apaches attacked Grade and his men," Matthew said. "In revenge for the murder of the Apache women and children."

"After the raid the soldiers were tired from their morning kill," Yellow Cloud said. "They rested. That is when the Apaches attacked. Grade and I and the other men came upon the murderers at about the same moment. The Apaches caught us all completely unaware."

Yellow Cloud put his arm on Matthew's shoulder. "That is why you must tell me about the raid," he said softly.

"When did you leave camp?" asked Matthew.

"At midday. I told the Captain I was going to bring back a rabbit or two for the men. I never went back. I could not. I have lived against my people for too long now. After this . . ." he pointed to the creek, ". . . I could take no more."

"So *that's* why Captain Grade came over to our tent. When you didn't come back, he suspected what you'd done. That you'd probably warn the Apaches. So he came up with a new plan, one you'd know nothing about."

"And you know of this plan," said Yellow Cloud.

Matthew sighed and clutched himself. He suddenly felt very cold. "If I tell you, my friend Zeke will die. If I don't, dozens more Indians will die. I want to help, Yellow Cloud, but what good will it do? Maybe the best thing for the Apaches to do is to let the white man share the land. It would end the killing, the hatred."

Yellow Cloud knelt and picked up a handful of dirt. "Is that what Grade told you? He just wants to 'share' the land?" He laughed harshly.

"I was raised by a white woman," Yellow Cloud went on. "I went to your schools from the time I was a young man. I studied hard. For a time I hated the Indian more than the white man. I wanted to be a doctor. To be a rich man. But since I could speak English as well as my native tongue, I was sent out here. To help resettle the Indian. Take him off his soil.

"Look at this soil. A hundred miles west of here, there is soil much like this. And beneath it there is gold. As near as the government can make out, there is a wealth of it. And it will do for this territory what the gold has done for the white man in California. In five years time there may be a thousand people standing where we are right now. Rich men, most of them. And they may never be aware that their good fortunes were found at the expense of the Indian."

"But it doesn't have to be like that. In California—"

"In California the Chumash and the Gabrieleno Indians populated the shores. They stood atop the soil where the gold lay buried. But when the white man came and found the gold, he pushed the Indian back further and further. Many that left died, and those who would not leave were killed. The government made treaties. But whenever they found something they wanted on the land, they broke their promises. Just as they are doing here."

It was hard for Matthew to hear the truth. But Yellow Cloud continued to tell his story. "People said that the gold in California ran like rivers. But the blood also ran like rivers. The blood of my people . . . *your* people, my brother."

What a strange expression. Matthew had never heard an Indian call him "brother." He knew he was part-Indian, but he had always felt like a white man. Always thought of himself as a white man.

As Matthew listened to Yellow Cloud, he felt strangely lost and found at the same time. Suddenly his drive to bathe himself in gold seemed to fall away. And for the first time in his whole life, he felt a true kinship with an Indian. Not admiration, but something rooted deep in his soul. This feeling made him calm and peaceful.

At the same time he felt as though he could not completely cut off his white heritage. The fact remained that he was both a white man and a red man. And that made him feel lost and alone.

Zeke had made *his* decision. Now Matthew would have to make his. Yellow Cloud was forcing him to make a choice. And no matter what choice he made, he'd be betraying a part of his heritage. Matthew was learning just how unfair life could be.

Finally he looked up at Yellow Cloud and said, "I'll tell you. I'll tell you about the raid. But we've got to warn Zeke."

"There is no time for that now," Yellow Cloud said. "We will have to put it into the hands of the Spirit. And you and I will have to do our best to see that no harm comes to your friend."

Death by the River

At dusk later that day, Matthew and Yellow Cloud waited and watched. Then they caught their first glimpse of Zeke marching the Apache leaders toward a small grove of trees. Matthew's heart began to pound. Everything was still working according to Grade's plan. Zeke appeared to be stiff and nervous. But he did not have to be very convincing as a magic man. Thanks to Matthew, the Apaches were well prepared for his arrival.

Because Matthew knew of the plan, he could spot where Grade and his men were lying in wait. Matthew thought it was almost funny how obvious the soldiers were. By contrast, the Apaches seemed to be nowhere in sight. It was as though they were invisible. From where he was, Matthew could see Captain Grade quite clearly. And almost as soon as Matthew spied the captain, he saw another man crouching beside him. Matthew had never seen this man before. But he was sure he knew who he was.

The man was not one of Grade's men. He was not in uniform. In the falling light, Matthew could just make out a fringed buckskin jacket. He knew it was the same buckskin jacket he had heard Captain Grade mention.

Matthew froze in terror. Captain Grade was kneeling beside Jeb Harlan. The bounty hunter who had been chasing Zeke all the way from Missouri was right here!

Matthew uttered a muffled curse. He realized now that the captain had never intended to let Zeke go free. He was just using him. After the raid, he would hand Zeke over to Harlan. And no doubt get part of the reward money, Matthew thought.

All was quiet except for the wind rushing through the trees. Now and then a few angry crows squabbled and snapped at one another.

Crickets, anxious for the night, began to chirp. But the men in the grove made no sound.

A snapping twig was the only warning the Apaches gave. And suddenly, the grove was filled with whoops, hollers, and war cries. The Indians dropped from the trees, and sprang from the bluffs and bushes.

Arrows and gunshots quickly filled the air. As planned, two warriors on horseback swooped down on Zeke. Then they quickly dragged him through the river and away from the fight.

Matthew saw Jeb Harlan emerge from the woods and aim his rifle at Zeke. He had a clear shot. But just then a loud gunshot rang through the trees on the bluff. Matthew's gun was still smoking when Yellow Cloud looked down and saw Harlan fall to his knees. Then both men watched him slump over— dead. Matthew closed his eyes and muttered a prayer. He felt sick to his stomach.

The other soldiers, seeing that they were outnumbered quickly began to retreat. But Captain Grade held his ground. "Stand and fight!" he cried bitterly to his men. "Stand and fight!"

He raised his gun and fired twice as the Indians advanced. Those two shots brought down two Apache warriors. But those were the last two shots the captain ever fired. As he reloaded his revolver, a dozen arrows found their way into Grade's chest. The captain screamed in pain and then fell backward over a tree stump.

Matthew turned away. But he could still hear the fading cries of the Indians as they ran after the retreating soldiers. Most of the soldiers rode off to safety. But four others, besides Harlan and Captain Grade, lay on the grassy carpet of the grove. Nearby lay the bodies of the two Indians Grade had killed.

Matthew stood atop the bluff and looked down at Zeke. They seemed to notice each other at the same moment. Matthew waved. A dazed but grateful Zeke waved back. But Matthew could see that Zeke was more interested in the man in the fringed buckskin jacket who lay in silence near a large rock.

Matthew watched as Zeke rolled Harlan over to make sure he was dead. Zeke could not seem to believe his eyes. Matthew thought he heard him say, "It's all over. My God, it's all over."

The soldiers had all seen Zeke carried away. They would assume he was killed by the Indians. Harlan and Grade were both dead. Zeke was free now.

But Matthew knew it was far from over. It would not be over for the Apaches. More soldiers would arrive. And the fighting would continue. More men, red and white, would lose their lives. And if Yellow Cloud was right, the White Man would eventually win. The Indians would have to give up this land and move to a new place. Then even *that* land would be taken from them.

And what of Matthew and Yellow Cloud? Matthew was sure that the soldiers would soon realize they had been betrayed. The soldiers knew that both men had vanished from camp on the same day. They would know that both of them helped the Apaches plan their attack. Matthew Wilder and Yellow Cloud would be hunted men for a long, long time.

Night soon fell. Matthew found himself staring at the same moon and stars he had pondered a week ago. Yet they were not the same. For those stars were the stars a young man makes wishes on. And that moon was the one a young man sings to, drunk on its rays. But tonight, for Matthew Wilder, the stars were nothing more than lights in the sky. And the moon was just something that shines on the coyotes to make them howl.

2450